He Wasn't a Stranger

by **DAWN LYNK-JONES**

RoseDog❖Books

PITTSBURGH, PENNSYLVANIA 15222

RoseDog Books
701 Smithfield Street
Pittsburgh, PA 15222
Visit our website at *www.rosedogbookstore.com*

ISBN: 978-1-4349-8895-9
eISBN: 978-1-4349-7887-5

*This book is dedicated to Annie Carol for believing in me,
to my family's love and support, and
to God, for always being by my side when I was in need.*

Table of Contents

Merry Christmas 1

Looking Back 7

The Here and Now 10

The Date 12

New Year's Eve 14

The Assault 16

2011...19

The Call that Saved Me...21

Disbelief...25

The Aftermath 27

The Now...30

Seek Help 32

Chapter 1: Merry Christmas

It's the time of year we can't wait for, when there's the brisk wind blowing against our skin. The snow lined streets and the silhouette of the trees danced on top of the snow. I long for the first real snow fall, the one that sparkles on the ground. It looks like tiny diamonds under the stars in the night sky. As a child I would lay awake, and gaze out at the snow, oh, how it sparkled! The winter is my favorite time of year. It's the time of love and giving. You celebrate the birth of Christ, and bond with your loved ones.

> **Luke: 2:10-11.** *"But the angel said to them, 'Do not be afraid. I bring you good news of great joy that will be for all the people.'"*

It's a time to be happy and embrace your children, so I thought! This year my past rose up and was looking at me in the face. As my daughter and I searched the stores of our neighborhood mini mall for small gifts and tokens to give away at Christmas Dinner, the kid's teachers, and of course, to family members, you really don't want to give gifts. You do it, because you're supposed to forgive and display your Christian side. We walked into the drug store; the line was up to the back of the store. People were everywhere, buying last—minute Christmas gifts, drinks, and eggnog. We collected want we wanted and went to the pharmacy counter, only two people ahead of us! I'm thinking, *Yes, we'll be out in five.*

My daughter and I made some small talk, as with most college freshmen, she wasn't really listening unless money is being exchanged. I paid for the items, and we made our way back up to the front. Upon exiting, we laughed about our favorite commercial of the women in the store singing Christmas songs into holiday cards as it recorded her singing, "Christmas is here, Fa la la la la, Christmas is here." We laughed as we sung our way outside!

When we turned by the corner, I came face to face with the man who had raped me 20 years ago! My heart started beating as our eyes became fixed on each other. I just couldn't breathe, like now as I recall it all. My legs had a mind of their own. They' wanted to run.

"Ma, what's wrong?"

I can't speak; I could only hear the pounding of my heart in my ears. "Come on, keep going, that's him, the one who raped me."

"Where? What does he look like?" She was jumping up and down trying to look through the store window.

All I wanted was to get to the car, I also kept looking back to see if he was there. During my last glance, he was there looking around to see where we were. In the car, I was still breathing heavily as flashes of my attack came back like it had just happened. I remembered everything that I spent twenty years trying to forget. My daughter asked me so many questions all at once,

"What's his name? Where is he? Do you see him?"

"There, in front of the store, talking on his phone, and looking around trying to see if we saw him." I tried to get out of the parking lot, but a lady was in the way. She wouldn't move her car fast enough. I didn't want him to get my license plate number. We had to back out, I saw him watching, the fear that overcame me. I was shaking!

We stayed only a few blocks away from the drug store, I pulled in the garage and we went into the house. My husband was cooking, I told him, "I saw him, the guy who raped me."

He saw the fear in my eyes, I was scared. I haven't thought about that night in a long, long time. My husband held me, and as always he made me laugh to help ease my fear.

That night I stayed up late, remembering how I struggled to break free from him. With his hands around my neck, I couldn't breathe. Why was he doing this to me is what I thought at that time. I lost consciousness for a few seconds, he shook me violently, and then those words he spoke that night, echoed in mind. He said, "I'll kill you if you tell!"

Here I am, thinking about the worst thing that ever happened to me. How I almost went mad. I spent two years in a state of non-existence. I didn't have a car then, so I could only call the Rape Crisis Hot Line and talk to them over the phone, and try to understand why he would do that to me. I wanted to die! I wanted to end my life. I wasn't ready for this life-changing experience. You would be surprised at how many women are raped every day. Many women don't tell anyone about it; they fear of what people would say or think of them; how they will be treated. I know this because it is what I was thinking when it happened to me.

I looked at my daughter who is so beautiful, but she too has that air about herself that I once had. I tried to prepare her for the worst in people, especially men. You never know what their real intentions are. I fear she, too, will one day experience this horrendous act from those who lurk in between two worlds, one of madness and the other of day to day existence.

I remember thinking that if I ran into him again. I would just walk up to him and ask him, "Why? Why did you rape me?" I wonder what his response would be or would he try to frighten me again.

For years now, I had dismissed the whole event, I have moved on with my life. I am self-confident again, I have a career, three children and I am actually happy. Seeing him jarred my subconscious baggage that was hidden, and out of view for some time now. Just seeing his face again, brought back that fear I had forgotten about.

I used to be afraid of my shadow! I wouldn't come outside, for fear of him getting me. I know it was God, who led me through it all. He carried me, because I can't walk.

In church, God revealed His self to me; he told me I would be fine. I was with my boyfriend, James, and his mother. I was thinking, *I want to die* and I want to kill myself. Just then the entire congregation stopped, no one was moving. I looked around, and I saw smoke, at least I thought it was smoke. It was Jesus floating towards me with clouds around His feet. He held His hand out for me to hold, I kissed it. He said "You'll be fine." I looked around to see if anyone else could see Him, His eyes, His mouth; it was as if they spoke without moving. He descended the same way He came, and disappeared into thin air. I will never forget how He held my hand in my time of need.

> In **Matthew 6:33-34**, -it says, *"But seek first his kingdom and his righteousness, and all these things will be given to you as well. Therefore do not worry about tomorrow, for tomorrow will worry about itself. Each day has enough trouble of its own."*

Memories are like flashes of light; they come and go with random scenes like a movie. I started remembering everything; how it all unfolded. In and out, man, these flashes of my tormentor came and went as I tried to get ready for Christmas dinner at my cousin's this year. I tried to hide what I was thinking; I really needed to feel the closeness of my family now more than ever. That's not going to happen, because we are all so distant.

What I wanted most was to go back to the other night the twenty-third of December, and relive the entire event. I would have gone to another store, stayed home or asked my husband to go. That way I wouldn't have run into him. It always brings such negative emotions within me, when our paths cross.

I remember ten years earlier, the time when I was driving down 7 Mile headed to my mom's house. As always when I go visit, she would have a detailed list of items she needed from the store. So, before my visit could start, I was off to the store. I pulled into the Food and Liquor Store's parking lot and parked. I went in. Once inside there was about ten maybe twelve people. Freezer doors slammed here and there. The punching of the key on the lottery machine echoed through-out. I walked the aisles quickly, gathered what my mother needed. Jumped in line, and waited for my turn.

Ring! Ring! went the bell over the door. I guess it was there so the owner would know if anyone entered while he was at the back of the store. With a glance to the right, there he was walking in. My heart was beating faster than a drum. My eyes were fixed on the man behind the protective glass. I wanted to leave everything behind, and run out. Then all I heard was: "Next," in between each breath. "Next," once again, the pain and fear over took me, but I managed to say, "Camel shorts, please."

I looked around to see where he was. He was in line, two customers behind me. His grin was like a knife piercing my heart. I grabbed my bag and left. My hands shook, my breathing was heavy. The flashes of my attack flickered in my mind. His hands around my neck, his words rang inside my head like the bell at the store. Then he slammed me on the bed. I wanted to cry, I wanted to scream, to get out, to escape, but nothing came out of my mouth! My voice was gone.

When I returned from the store getting the items I left behind, all I could think of was getting the hell out of there, and going home to my apartment. I felt safe there, no one from the neighborhood knew where I lived or had my number. I said my goodbyes and left. The fear of him kept me away especially during the summer months.

The sound of my son's voice brought me back to the present, "Ma, Ma, we need to bake the cookies for Santa."

"What?"

"The cookies," he said in his big boy voice.

"I know, Edward." Cookies, these kids are worried about cookies, the last thing on my mind is Santa and some damn cookies.

I scanned the T.V. for a movie to watch. Wasn't anything really interesting or good on it, nothing that would hold my attention anyway. So, I started wrapping gifts in my bedroom. Most of the gifts were in the back of our closet. The kids never look there. It is about 2 A.M. now, and I can't sleep. When I'm on vacation, I never sleep, but now I really can't sleep. I kept on looking out the window to see if I recognize the cars driving up and down the street. *Did he follow us home, did he see my plate?* The main question in the back of my mind was, Will he come after me again?

It's Christmas Eve, and we usually have an anniversary party or dinner, but not this year. My mind and heart weren't into it. I felt happy and worried at the same time. I didn't want to do anything or go anywhere. The kids wanted us to have another Wii Party like the previous year. I was tired and grateful to have them, I just wanted to be with them, and watch how happy they all were.

My daughter likes to walk through the house and make random noises and yelling at the top of her voice and her brothers are not far behind her. Our house is noisy and a complete adventure. Our home is a place for them to display their individuality that is until I can't take the noise and the mess anymore. Terry likes to remind me that I am hard and unemotional most of the time. If she could see in my soul, and see what made me this way then she would change the words that she likes to float through the air like the sting you feel after a bee has branded you with its stinger.

My anniversary came and went like a sweet summer breeze. Not like the emotional roller coaster ride I have to endure many of the years before. My husband was a different person this year, not the ass he once was. My best friend now, that's a fucking trip. I thought I would never say that shit.

It's Christmas!! I love Christmas. This year I tried so hard to let go of my own baggage and just give to everyone I could, that is without bringing in the new broke as a joke. I brought gifts for everyone that would be at my cousin's this year. Even my evil ass aunt Karen was there, with her son, who is a mama's boy, you know, everyone has one. She is the type of person who is out to destroy any and everyone at any cost as long as she ends up on top. She thinks she is, but, she has blocked her own blessings. Anyway, back to the dinner. We got there early, and Mary wasn't completely done cooking dinner. So, I offered to help to make myself feel more comfortable. I fried the chicken, and Mary left to go pick up my mom and her mother. They live together in an apartment a few building down. They have been living together since I was about five, maybe seven.

Mary and I are not as close as we used to be, because of some things I said about her to my aunt. Well, she told her what we discussed. I hope you're thinking what I am, what a fucking snake? Right! We're trying to repair our damaged relationship if that's possible. Now, Mary and Karen are the best of friends because Karen told Mary she didn't have anything to say about her. That's a freaking lie; she said plenty over the years, too.

What's funny about black women is, truly deep down inside, they hate you for what do want to be, what you are trying to do, and for any accomplishments you make. It's only a few people around me that I truly feel who love me, and want the best for me.

After a half hour, Mary returned with everyone else and they sat around making small talk and taking about old times. Everyone was in good spirits, I as well, until Karen and her Carl arrived. She tried to get under my skin. They didn't speak. It angered me, but I tried to keep my anger inside me. I wanted to just leave. Karen blurts out, "The party can start now that I'm here." I wanted to vomit in my mouth.

We gathered around to bless the food, and then proceeded to eat, talk shit, and laugh about the past indirectly. Years ago, this would have been the best, because we are all together now. Now, I feel separate from them all, you know like an out of body experience, if I'm not really a part of this family. We usually take some pictures, but I didn't bring my camera on purpose. I didn't want take any pictures of them.

Everyone headed out shortly after that, but I stayed around with Mary for about twenty minutes. The kids and I left, and went home. I replayed the entire day over and over in my head. Remembering how much fun we all used to have. I missed it at that moment. At home, I'm at peace; our home is comfortable and holds the positive spirits of my loved ones. These people here love me and I them.

How would my life have been different is something I think about from time to time, 'Would it be better or worse? What would I be doing? Where would I be?'

I'm sitting down-stairs, in the living room. My memories that were buried deep in my subconscious suddenly flood like raging waves into view. My mind is the projector that is playing on the screen like at the movies; one after another set of images of my past gush forward. I turned to look over my shoulder and it's like I'm there all over again.

Chapter 2: Looking Back

I was nineteen, confident, and sexy. I have long, dark, brown hair, and beautiful skin, all the women in my family had beautiful skin. My grandmother said it was because of our Great, Great Grandparents who were Native-Americans. I intimidated women and men with my presence. I was cocky to some degree, but sure of what I wanted, if that's possible at twenty-one. I was dating James. I wanted him to marry me; because he was the first guy I dated who wanted more out of life. We went out to plays, concerts, etc.; he bought me things no other man had.

After some months in the relationship, things started to fizzle out. He wasn't available as much as before; he didn't want to talk to me anymore. I knew it was someone else. So, being so sure of that, I accepted another date with a guy from our neighborhood. Our families knew of each other. He ran with my cousins. I loved him from a far. He was a little older, but that didn't matter to me. He was every girl's dream in the neighborhood. I loved the idea of having him for my boyfriend.

I was at that age when you think you can take over the world, I was invincible. Carefree, and hanging out with my friends. Clubbing, trying to be grown. Not knowing what it really entails.

> **Romans: 12:2,** *"Do not conform any longer to the pattern of this world, but be transformed by renewing your mind. Then you will be able to test and approve what God's will is His good, pleasing, and perfect will."*

I wish I could say I learned this at an early age, but I couldn't. I did conform, and that's why life was hard for me.

I saw Damon all the time around the neighborhood. We would drive pass my house, and stop to talk, flirt, make sexual comments hidden, within his glances and through-out his words. I liked the attention he gave; I always wanted to date him. We tried dating a year before, which included talking on the phone, and yes, we slept together once. It wasn't what I thought it would be like with him. He didn't stir my desires that were within me. Basically he was boring in bed. He wanted us to get together again but, I wouldn't sleep with him again. I thought it was a waste of time. I never told him, because of how I felt about him.

People are surprised when a woman says, "He wasn't a stranger, I had known him since I was ten years old, and he was my friend."

How quick do we forget that by nature some men have animalistic characteristics. They watch their prey and wait for the perfect time to ambush and then destroy. We never see it coming! We live in an unrealistic world of Barbie Dolls, and Easy-Bake Ovens. I didn't learn this until much later on that some of them can be demons that walk among us.

So you see when three years have passed and he was in my view again, I didn't think things would spiral out of proportion. With Scorpio's, you think you can control it all. Going out with him and his friends wouldn't hurt. James won't know; I could have my cake and eat it, too! So I thought. Little did I know that this would change my life forever.

My family is no different; I mean the women in our family didn't prepare us young girls for what awaited us outside the home. We were defenseless against the disruptive impulses that lay hidden behind the smile of men.

Sometimes, researchers make reference that some urban families are unable to function emotionally or as a social unit. This dysfunctional behavior is perpetuated from one generation to the next. Oh, it is passed on, believe it. It's true. When children watch their parents argue and fight, what do you think they do when they grown up? They find someone to argue and fight with. When they see a loving and supportive family, they learn to be loving and supportive later in life.

I say this to ask from whom does a rapist learn from? Who did they see get raped? Is it hereditary? What makes them want to hurt women? Why us? Why me? So many questions went through my mind. I didn't deserve what he did to me; he took my power, my spirit. I was broken for many years, to some extent I still am.

You see, black girls, we grow up believing that a knight in shining armor will gallop up on his white horse and rescue us (from our dysfunctional families, sex, boys, parents, and relationships) from the things set in place to really destroy us. We are reared to do things that would please the would-be suitor. We are taught to cook, clean, and take care of babies and siblings. These qualities- in a woman make you more marketable.

I wasn't like most girls, and I acted completely different from many. I wasn't caught up in the looks or trying to be someone I was not. At twenty-two, I possessed a more womanly look that accompanied my model-like features. I could stand toe to toe with the best of them. I wanted to be seen by all, and when about ten of us from the neighborhood decided to get together to hang out, I was for it.

He Wasn't a Stranger

My boyfriend was still behaving as if I wasn't good enough to marry him. He was an arrogant ass, and I wanted to see the other side of things; and waiting on him, I refused to do. I decided to go, too. I went to my girls, Margarita's house, and I had a two piece suede skirt and jacket outfit on. I had on my black suede shoes. Man, I looked good! So, when we walked outside and all the guys looked, all at once I heard, "Damn Donna." I smiled, because I thought I was hot and so did they!

I didn't know Damon would be there. Mark pulled up first, "Donna, you can ride with me if you want."

I said, "Okay." Before getting in, I looked at Damon, and he at me. The look spoke for its self, he motioned me to his car but I got in Mark's. We went to a club and had a few drinks. Mark hit on me a bit throughout the night. It meant nothing to me.

Damon called me that night, totally unexpected. I didn't think he still had my mom's number. He pushed up hard and quick. He disliked the fact the Mark had first crack at me, but would I take the bite.

"He is a punk and he ain't shit, he knows who killed his best friend and he didn't do anything." He was so jealous, and he blasted Mark the entire conversation. This turned me off.

"He still has no game",' I said to myself. If only he had spoken of different things, maybe us getting together finally, I would have nibbled on his line he dangled in a heartbeat.

So, I did what most girls did then, I went for the other guy. I dated him briefly; only to find out the he had a girlfriend and a child that he lived with. Males, they will try anything to get what they want from you. Women, too, don't get me wrong. Both sexes tend to do what we want at times instead of what we need. Not all, but must women accept whatever men dish out. We want the knight in shining armor, no matter what's really on the inside. We're all caught up in the fantasy! I knew I had no place in his relationship other than being his 'sometime' lover. I gracefully bowed out and just stopped calling him. It took a minute, because I didn't want to be just his lover. I was worthy of so much more.

Chapter 3: The Here and Now

Still sitting in the living room, jolted back to reality by the tapping sound of the sticks hitting together before they violently smashed into the drum set we gave the boys for Christmas, "1, 2, 3, 4, bang, bang, boom, and bang!"

My son carried on for about a good five minutes, "I'm making music, Mama." I immediately moved away, but the loud banging vibrated through the entire downstairs.

I headed in the kitchen, "That damn drum set has to go in the basement as soon as possible, what the hell was I thinking getting that?" I've been talking to myself a lot lately, and I seem to just blurt out things as I move through the house.

Terry's birthday is today, the twenty-seventh of December; she wants to have a party and a sleep over. She just turned nineteen! Wow, where did the years go? Here I am reliving the past moment by moment. My attack fast-forwarded over and over to the same scene, in the same part that nearly destroyed me twenty years ago. Her cousins came over and we played "Just Dance" on the Wii. That diverted my thoughts for a good hour before my husband and I headed out for dinner.

I feel different; it is as if I'm stuck in this state of hollowed existence. My world has been turned up-side-down. I can't believe I felt safe, and that I blocked all this out of my mind all these years. Just one glance at him, just one stare opened the gates of years of the torment I felt when I as a young woman.

As if I wasn't already lost in a world of perplexity, we went to the movies to see *Colored Girls* by Tyler Perry. The movie disrupted my thoughts and magnified my own attack. The pain and fear she felt, I, too, know it well. One character was raped, just like me. It was like seeing myself there on the screen. It was a bit overwhelming sitting there watching it all. All I could see was it was me sitting there, hiding in my room. The rape of one, the abuse of the other, the lies uncovered by the mother, all deliberately sprung forth my own pain I had concealed within me all these years.

You see, she knew her attacker, just like I did. I searched my mind and tried to see what she did, if she made a gesture that made him think it was okay. I played it over, and over: was it her fault? Was it mine? Did we silently ask for it without understanding what we really wanted? Men use us, because we allow them too. I often think of one of my favorite authors, Zeale Nell Hurston. In her novel, *They Eyes are Watching God,* she refers to women as mules of this world. I completely understand that statement now. We carry everything around on our backs that men, society, and life give us. We spend our entire existence trying to find that perfect love, relationship, and at the same time understand our place in the cosmic scheme of things.

Chapter 4: The Date

A few weeks passed and I was back and forth between my mom's and my boyfriend's house. Leaving, staying, crying, arguing, and just plain fucking lonely! At my mom's, I always had a sense of freedom, uninterrupted play, and movement. Seeing Damon caught my curiosity. He was so handsome, he had the whitest teeth. If I only knew he would be the one who would try to destroy me. So you see, "He Wasn't a Stranger" he was someone I've known since I was ten years old.

Ring, ring, ring! I grabbed the phone on the third ring. "Hello."

"Hey, you want to hang out tonight, Donna?" His voice floated through the air into the phone.

"Sure," I said. James wasn't interested in seeing me. "Pick me up at around eight...on second thought, I will come over there at around six. My aunt is over there and I will get her to drop me off on her way home." I thought to myself, *This way James won't know where I went. I can date Damon and start building a relationship with him in case we break up.*

I laid around the house waiting until it was time to get ready. We all talked and laughed in the living room. Everyone was moving about the house. The one thing I loved and hated about our beat-up house was that we didn't have a lot but we were content with what we have. Whenever anyone came over, we all came out of our perspective spots like ants scrambling from the whole in the ground and migrated to the center point of the house-the living room. There's music playing in the background from the commercial playing on the T.V., cigarette smoke filled the air, and the aroma of fried chicken cooking in the kitchen tempted our empty bellies.

I hated our way of living or should I say the way we survived in the socio-economic scheme of things. I wanted so much more, but I didn't know how to go about getting it.

My mother wanted Karen to go by the gas company and drop off a payment in the drop box. "Donna, come on I'm getting ready to go," Karen yelled upstairs.

"Okay!" I yelled back. I had already pulled Karen aside when she entered the house and asked her to give me a ride. She agreed, but you always had to give her gas money. She was so damn cheap! I got dressed and headed downstairs. They were still sitting around exchanging comments, and laughs.

"Well, I'm about to go." Karen blurted into the midst of the conversation. I grabbed my coat and followed close behind.

As we pulled out the driveway, and headed towards the corner, "Donna, where am I dropping you at?" Karen stated.

I returned the answer quick and with a smile to accompany it, "On Gilchrest across from MichCon."

"Who's house?"

"Damon's."

"I don't need a ride home; he's going to take me home later."

"All right," Karen said softly.

We pulled up in front of his house. He had his own place. He worked for the Big Three, because his father did. He helped him get in.

I loved the idea of having a guy with his own place. I thought to myself as I stepped on the porch and rang the bell. The door opened and there he was, greeting me with that handsome smile of his. Little did I know I was looking at danger directly in the face.

Chapter 5: New Year's Eve

It's January the thirty-first, New Year's Eve, and over the past week I haven't be able to think of anything else but this horrible monster. I can't sleep; I might have had about a good six hours over the last two to three days. The anxiety that has built up in me is ridiculous. I don't know what to do, I wanted to bring in the New Year in Church with my cousins and my family but I just didn't want to leave the house.

My mind is racing back and forth, different parts of the attack, his eyes, his hands, and the bewildered look flashing across my face as it all happened.

I'm forty-two years old now. I have to be strong to protect my children. How can I tell them, I'm scared, I can't make love right now because I keep seeing my attacker's face. Click, click, and click. The ticking seems so loud as I looked up at the clock, I remembered I have a hair appointment late this afternoon, and the fresh air and the ride might do me some good. I finally got dressed and went to the car. The drive wasn't more than ten minutes. Once inside the shop I sank down in the chair and closed my eyes. I hoped she would wash everything down the drain with the suds from my hair.

My hair looked good after it was done, it always does. I headed home. I am becoming paranoid; I keep looking in at the cars passing by. Watching the cars behind carefully, making sure they hadn't been behind me too long. I stopped at the A.T.M., and went home. I find myself staring at everyone, making sure it's not him.

I started dinner as soon as I set my coat down, any and everybody who knows me knows I don't cook. My husband cooks all the time. I am spoiled when it comes to that. I really must be fucked up in the head to be cooking anything. I keep asking myself, "What if I could do it all again?" The interesting detail or fact is that by changing that negative incident would change my entire life as I know it now. It could all be different, and do I want that. I am who I am now, because of the things I experienced in life. I think I'm a pretty good person and I am confident and strong.

I'm sitting around thinking about my past and my present, listening to my kids in the other room watching WWE Smack Down.

"Whhooooo, get in the ring, Triple H!" Edward yells out. Those babies are serious about their wrestling! This is my life; my New Year will be spent with them here in our home where I have been safe for eleven years.

The winter darkness is quickly ascending upon the day, and my thoughts are keeping me from enjoying my holiday this year. My Christmas season has been destroyed by a rapist who still walks the streets free! He moves carefree and I'm sure he awaits for another opportunity to strike again. How many women is it now? Has he raped five, ten or maybe many more? I think I was his first, and there was a rumor of a second victim shortly after me. The entire neighborhood buzzed about it. My girl Carol called me and told me that some-one had posted flyers about him being a rapist. The flyers had a picture of him on them, and it warned me about him.

It has been said that once a rapist rapes, he can't stop. The rapist needs to be in control, they needs to demonstrate his strength on the victim, and it makes him feel powerful.

I have to return to work in a few days; I think that's going to be good for me. I need to keep busy to block as much of these images of my past that are moving through my mind like a flash from a digital camera. With each click of the button, I remember more from my childhood, my life as a teenager, and my attack. That's what I want to hide in the darkest corner of my mind. I never want it to resurface again, it eats at me each and every time I see him.

What if I flip the script and find him first, I could call in a few flavors and get his address, and ride past his home and plan my attack on him. I could just expose him with flyers and ads in the paper like his other victims did; it would shatter his world. I could take the law into my own hands, and plan his end and make him disappear just like I did that night. He needs to know how painful being raped is; I could appear out of nowhere and rape him again and again. He needs to feel what his victims feel.

Would this make me a monster, too? Would the Lord be displeased with me because I didn't forgive this trespass against me? I would only know when judgment day is before me. Will the Lord reveal his undying love for me again by appearing before my eyes to assure me that all will be fine? As I move about in my unconscious cloud of mixed pieces of reality and my waking death, I know that in my heart it is the spirit of Jesus that carries me.

The New Year's Eve special echoed throughout my bedroom, "5-4-3-2-1, Happy New Year!" went hundreds of voices and screams as it exploded through the television. My thoughts were fast-forwarded back to the present with my husband and the kids. We all hugged and kissed and said "Happy New Year."

The night ended well, and as we settled down to rest, but not before we keep our promise to watch *Toy Story 3* with the boys. My first promise in 2011 will be to continue to be a good mother even if I feel I'm losing my mind.

Chapter 6: The Assault

I waited for him to open the screen door; I returned a grin that matched his. My aunt pulled off and turned the corner. I walked in, "Hey, what's up?"

"You, finally," he said. I should have recognized what that meant. I didn't see the warning signs-they were everywhere.

"Come on in the back, I'm watching T.V." We headed back to his room. I sat on the edge of the bed. There wasn't a chair. We made small talk and laughed a little. "Are you hungry?" I replied with a yes.

"We can order some pizza, and head to the store before it comes."

He picked up the phone, "Hello Big T's Pizza," someone said from the other end of the phone said in a loud voice.

"Can I get a large pizza with everything on it?"

"Sure, that'll be $15.85, pick up or delivery?"

"Delivery" he said.

"What's your address?" the women stated.

"It's 19723 Gilchrest."

"That will be about twenty minutes, sir."

"All right." He hung up the phone.

"Let's go to the store."

"Okay," I said. We went up front and grabbed our coats and went out the door. The store was only two blocks away. We got there quick, he got some beer and me a pop. We might have been gone about ten minute's tops. We went in the house and headed to his room to wait for the pizza. He sat with his head in my lap; I stroked his head, mainly his eyebrows. His eye brows were dark and thick, he was so handsome, and I can't believe I was there with him.

We ate the pizza and I picked all the onions and mushrooms off. *I hate onions and mushrooms,* I thought to myself in between bites. We watched some random shows on T.V., and talked much about nothing. I didn't want to sleep with him but I wanted to be there with him. I wanted to kiss, and fondle one another, but not have sex! I guess I should have thought about this more before coming, before doing the things I did.

I was wearing a shirt and jeans, and he was wearing shorts and T-shirt.

"Can I have some shorts and a top?" I said.

"Yeah, hold on, let me find something," he said with a smile. It was about 8 or 8:30 in the evening now. I changed in the bathroom, and walked back into his. He was laying in the bed, waiting for me to come over to him. I got in next to him under the covers. He held me so tight, and loved the way I felt in his arms. He turned me around and kissed me passionately. I returned it just the same. We went at it for about thirty minutes, touching, pumping against one another, and in and out of each other's clothes. "Man, I want you; I can't keep doing this and not get any."

He started pulling down my shorts forcefully, "No, no, wait a minute," but he continued to pull on my panties harder and harder. I gripped them so hard saying, "No." He pulled my panties off from my body so hard my legs jerked from the act. Finally, the light went off in my head, *Oh my God, he's coming to rape me!* "No, no, wait a minute, Damon."

"What? You gonna give me some?"

Those words buzzed through the room, my head like a chain-saw. I was scared; it was too late to be scared. This was really happening to me. I tried to prevent the act from being concluded, I blurted out, "Okay, okay, do you have some condoms? I'm not on the pill. I don't want to get pregnant!"

"Yeah, hold on I get them out the other room." He walked out and I jumped up and grabbed my pants. I tried to get them all the way on before he came back. He came in naked with the condom on this erect penis and saw me, "What! You are giving me some pussy." He grabbed me so fast, before I had a chance to think.

His hands were around my throat, squeezing the life out of me, and it felt like I lost consciousness for a second or two. I couldn't breathe; he body slammed me on the edge of the bed. It hurt so badly! I couldn't scream, he pulled my pants off and took me. He thrust his penis inside, and with each pump he said, "It's so good, girl you have so good stuff." I laid there afraid to scream, yell, I couldn't speak. In and out he pushed until he came, and rolled off me.

I got up slowly, "Where you going?" he said.

"Bathroom"

"Oh, you wanted it you know you did!" I walked in the bathroom and closed the door, trying to play it cool so I could get out of there before he rapes me again. He opened the door, and gave me a wash cloth, he was star-ing at me, and my eyes were filled with tears. I don't want him to see that. I was afraid I wouldn't escape this nightmare alive. He kept walking pass the door, I knew he was thinking now about what he just did. I was scared!

I came out and got my clothes and went back in to put them on. He watched me so hard, saying nothing at the moment. Once, I was dressed he blurted out, "What are, you going to tell people? What you going to say? I did-n't rape you!"

"I know" I tried to say with a convincing voice. He didn't buy it. I headed towards the front room, he grabbed and pushed against the wall, my body trembled with fear!

"If you tell anyone, I'll kill you!"

I just kept my mind on getting out of there. "It's okay, Damon. Come on and take me home before I get in trouble." I tried not to look at him; he would know it was a lie. He just might kill me. He raped me, so at this point he just might kill me. Everyone knows him and, he didn't want anyone to know he was a rapist! Damon got dressed and came back up to the living room.

I tried to open the door, he was behind me and he put his hands around my neck. "Donna, I'll kill you if you tell!" I thought he was going to just kill me then, but he opened the door and let me out. I wanted to run up the street.

So many thoughts went through my mind, *Be cool and get home alive.* I was quiet during the ride: it was the longest ride in the world. He pulled up in front of my house, I reached for the door handle, he grabbed me again.

"You better not tell!"

And my reply was, "I won't."

He loosened his grip, and I got out. He got out too, "Donna, I'm sorry. I didn't mean to."

I was home, I was safe now, I turned around and finally looked at him in his eyes and said, "Don't you ever speak to me again."

I ran towards the porch, he stood there watching me. I went in and went upstairs to my room. I laid across the bed and cried for which seemed like hours. I came down once to shower, I wanted to wash the pain, hurt, and the smell of him off me. I didn't tell that night!

When I closed my eyes, I see what I helped him do to me over and over again. I almost committed suicide that night.

Chapter 7: 2011

It's New Year's Day, and I got right up and started taking down the Christmas tree and lights. Like all kids they weren't too happy to help out, but the boys did remove all the Christmas bulbs from the tree. That made things a lot faster! I was trying to get the kids ready for the school week, when my girl Janette left me a text to come over and have a drink and catch a movie. I was glad to get the invite, I really needed to get out of the house, and the kids could have a play date as well.

Janette and I sat in her kitchen, and the kids went upstairs to the bedroom to play the Xbox. "Janette, I came face to face with the guy who raped me years ago at the drug store."

"What! What did you do?" Janette asked.

"I panicked, and almost started running."

"Oh, Donna, I'm so sorry," she spoke softly as her eyes filled with tears.

"Please don't cry, because I will. I haven't cried about this in years," I said. "I'm afraid all over again, and every time I see him, the attack emerges in my mind, and the fear overwhelms me."

We went downstairs and watched a movie while we sipped on some Margaritas. Jeanette couldn't drink them. I put a little too much salt in them, and she made Apple Martini. I felt a little better, but unsure of what to do next. It was around 11:00 P.M. and I told her we were going to head home. I thanked her for listening, and for being a friend. We started for home, which was only five to seven minutes away.

I got undressed, and headed in the bedroom, my thoughts were clouded with the things I did wrong leading up to the attack. I made some wrong choices, and I wished I was wiser then, because I wouldn't still have these horrible thoughts going through my mind all the time.

I have a good life, I'm happy. I don't want to relive being raped every time I see him. I wonder what he thought when he saw me; did he regret his part in it at all? Does he fear me and what I might possible do to him? I won't ever know unless I confront him. Am I mentally capable of handling this confrontation? These are some things I asked myself.

I have spent too much time living in fear. Hiding what happened from everyone, you see you don't want outsiders to see how vulnerable you really are. I didn't want people to talk about me, and about what happened. I didn't want people to think differently of me.

I thought that I could control the situation, and him. Young women just don't realize how naïve they really are. We don't understand that for some men this is a daily routine, they have done this a number of times, and women play a bigger part in it than what they really know.

I wanted to tell my story, because it's time for me to release this pain, this guilt I have buried deep within my soul. I can't continue to fall apart whenever I see him. We live in the same city, but our paths don't cross that often; but I refuse to allow him to destroy the positive rhythm I flow to now.

I want to warn women, I want them to examine their own actions. They need to make sure they too are not helping another man crust their entire existence. If you aren't taught how to be proactive in your own life, you don't know that you are the one who is causing the structure to fall when you try to erect it. We have to make a choice, it's them or us.

It has been almost two weeks since our paths crossed, and I still can't sleep. I had to take sleeping pills to relax and get a few hours of sleep. I'm tense and I pray that on my trip to the grocery store or the gas station that he won't be standing there in front of me waiting to see how I react. I have to do something to liberate my soul, that's been locked in chaos for over twenty years.

I can't even function intimately with my husband right now, I don't want to be touched, looked at, or kissed. I want us to be able expressed the intimacy we once did we used to have with one another, how can you do that when you see or hear something that jars a painful part of your past taking away your future.

Chapter 8: The Call That Saved Me

After hours of contemplating my own death, I decided to call my aunt for help! The phone rang several times before she finally answered. "Hello."

"Karen, Karen, what are you doing?" I managed to say as I sobbed.

"What's wrong?" she yelled into the phone.

"Damon raped me and I don't want anyone to know"

"What happened Donna, you have to go to the police!"

I explained that I didn't want to, because he threatened to kill me if I did, I said as my voice trembled with fear. Karen stated, "I'm on my way, you need to be ready!"

All I could hear was a dial tone, and I hung up the receiver. I got dressed and waited for her to come and get me. It seems as if hours had passed, and then she was at the door.

She talked at me the entire ride to the police station, I could hear bits and pieces of her words; but not completely. My heart was pounding so loud I could hear it in the ears. "I'm scared, I don't want to tell anyone," I said as the fear took over me. "Please don't make me go in there," I said as we parked in the parking lot of the 8th Precinct.

"You're going, get out of the car!" We walked in, all the officers standing around looked at us.

"Can I help you?" a voice spoke from behind the counter.

I whispered, "I need to file a report."

The officer, said "Okay" with great force. "What kind of report do you need to file?" the officer stated.

With tears in my eyes, I uttered, "Sexual assault." I tried to speak in a low voice because I didn't want anyone to hear me but they still did.

He gave me a strange look, "Sit over there; I'll be with you in a moment."

I felt that each and every person in the room heard me, and they could see what happened to me by just looking at me. I walked over to the table and sat down. My aunt went to the car and waited.

It only took him a few seconds to get his papers, a clipboard, and a pen. It felt like an eternity! I sat there and the looks people gave me as they too waited to file their reports. I turned my head and looked out the window because I was ashamed of being raped.

The police officer walked over and took the seat next to me, "Miss, I'm Officer Baker and I need you to tell me everything that happened so I can report it as accurately as possible."

I looked at him and said, "Okay."

"What's your name, address, phone, and your age?"

"My name is Donna Jones, I live at 19199 Huntsville, my phone number is 313-533-9776, and I am twenty-two years old."

Officer Baker was writing everything bit of information I gave about my attacker, the rape, and what happened before and after the rape. I had to sit through two hours of questions, and recalling every shameful part of my attack.

At the end I explained how afraid I was, because the guy lived in the neighborhood. "Officer Baker, he said he would to kill me if I told what he did to me. I believe he will, I almost didn't get out of there alive."

"Well, what do you want to do? I can call him and discuss the matter. I can explain if he comes near you again, we can pick him up."

I agreed to this course of action, because I didn't want anyone to know. It was the wrong thing to do; I let fear persuade me to keep it a secret. It only made things worse.

"I will call you with an update, when I speak to him," he stated. Before he left, he turned to me and said "You need to press charges!" He walked over to the desk and I headed outside to the car. I started crying as soon as I opened the door, my aunt looked at me not knowing what else to say. I cried so hard! We drove home in silent, neither of us speaking, my eyes fixed on the windshield with a thousand things running through my mind.

We pulled up in front of the house, as I blew out a long exasperated sign. Karen finally said something, "Are you going to tell them what happened? You can't keep it to yourself; it'll eat away at you!"

"I'm not going to tell anyone what happened," I said. "And thanks for going with me!" I slowly climbed out of the car, and headed inside. I felt like someone had just beat me down, and my body was lifeless. I quietly said out loud what I was thinking without realizing it, "When he calls him, he's going to come for me again."

I closed the door and walked up to the porch and went inside. Once upstairs I fell into a deep sleep, an undisruptive slumber. The morning came and went before I got up to eat, and the afternoon was fast upon us.

Knock, knock, knock. My mother went to the door, "Who is it?"

"Damon. Is Donna here?"

"Just a minute. Donna, someone's at the door!"

I wondered to myself, *Who could it be?* And I was so scared to go to the door. My heart was beating so fast the people down the street could hear it if they tried. I went to the window and looked out; it was him right there on the porch. I begged "Please, tell him I'm not here!"

My mom looked at me, "You tell him." Then she walked into the back of the house. I went to the door, and opened it wider. He looked crazy.

"Oh you went to the police, so what I did I tell you?" Before I could answer, Damon pulled out a .357 Magnum and pointed it at me. My mouth fell opened, I tried to scream but nothing came out! "I'm gonna kill you Donna, tell someone else." He turned and jumped off the porch, and ran to his car. He pulled off fast, and turned the corner. I stood there, my heart was pumping so fast I could barely breathe, and I wanted to hide; to get away from there. I had nowhere else to go!

I wanted to escape it all, my family, and him. I called my grandmother and asked her if I could come and stay with her for a while, she has always shown me love and kindness. My grandmother allowed me to come live with her, youngest daughter, my aunt, Karen, and her third eldest son, Gary. I wanted to put it all behind and it did with getting into WSU Extension Program in the city, and I wanted to change my future. This was the beginning, it had to start with me, and I didn't really know how to go about things, but thanks to one of my best girlfriends from high school; she helped me with the paperwork and the financial aide process. This was my chance to start a new beginning.

I attended class at the extension center class Monday through Friday for about three to four hours a day. I walked to the center, which was about a mile coming and a mile going. If I had any money I took the bus as far as I could go. I was allowed to sleep upstairs in the room with my aunt, but I didn't know how long this would last given the kind of person she could be. My aunt was there at the house but she was the kind of person at times she would do nothing for anyone but herself. So, on the day's she so felt like being selfish, I walked one foot in front of the other. I'm glad I have the determination to continue, because many people would have given up. I refused! I wanted to make something of my life.

I believe God brings people into your life for a reason and a season, and some are meant to stay and others are not. I know that God has aligned many angels around me to help guide me and protect me at different points in my life. I am grateful that I am an apple in His eye, because He has pulled me from darkest and saved me.

Hebrews 13:6, *"Never will I leave you; never will I forsake you."*

Starting college was a way for me to put my date rape behind me, and to make a move in the right direction. I was afraid to talk to people, to move about, to be me again. I learned to allow people to become my friends, and to smile again. To laugh at the things that struck me as being funny and I found my voice again and held my head up high. My transformation started.

After my first semester ended I earned a 3.5 G.P.A. I was so proud of myself, I was the second female to attend college. My aunt was the first but she didn't finish. It was like a slap in the face to watch your younger niece start college and you yourself didn't earn an associate's degree. When winter came again, and classes begun, I asked her to take me and she refused. I knew then if I wanted to go I had to walk! I walked through the snow, rain, and blistering sun. The good thing was, I met so many nice people and when they saw me walking in 2-3 inches of snow they gave me a ride. Clayton and Cary! These two showed me what friendship was, and I learned to trust that all men weren't like Damon. They would pick me up at my grandmother's house and we would ride to school if we had classes on the same days.

My aunt became pregnant, and I knew what that meant. After class one night my grandmother wanted to speak to me. "Donna, you're going to have to go back home," she stated in her motherly voice.

I said in a pleading, more like begging voice, "Why? I won't get in the way!"

She went on to tell me that Karen wanted me to leave, and she didn't want me upstairs in the room with her. I was so hurt, because I knew I would have to go back to the madness I came from.

I was hurt and I knew my grandmother's love for me bothered my aunt, Karen, it always did. I wanted to stay there where I felt safe, but she wanted me gone so I went. I packed my bags and went home, and I went back up to my room that I shared with my sister and my two cousins. I then realized how much I missed them. I loved them. It didn't seem to make a difference to my mother. They wanted to protect me, and keep me safe. I will never forget them for that.

A bus schedule is what I needed because I was going to keep going to college no matter what. I was out at the bus stop for hours sometimes, waiting to get to class. I came home the same way, because Clayton and Cary didn't live nearby anymore. I couldn't count on them this time, so I was on my own. Although I would see them in class, and they would offer to take me home, I wouldn't allow them to go out of their way to help me. I had to rely on myself!

Chapter 9: Disbelief

Here I am at swim practice with my kids and going over every event that happened with Damon. After the rape, how he came after me, my cousin, and how my family looked at me, their faces said it was my entire fault. "She liked him, and who knows he might not had raped her." I couldn't believe that thought about me. I haven't given much thought to any of this in years, and having to recall it everyday is a bit stressful. I don't want to remember, I want it to all just go away. I want to continue with my life as it was, and **live peacefully**!

> **Numbers: 6:26,** *"The Lord turns his face toward you and give you peace."*

It has caused a great void in me, and finally my way of fixing this problem is to write about it, and get it all out into the open after twenty years. I want to expose him, and let everyone know just what really happened. With every rapist, the story they tell is always to some degree different from the truth. With men, their favorite statement is: "You know she asked for it or she knew what she was doing." Oh, what about this statement, "She was a tease, so I gave it to her."

I became invisible to the eye; I didn't come outside for six months, not even to sit on the porch. If I did my aunt sat outside with me, not my mother. I think she secretly knew I was raped, but she seemed to have hated me for it. I was her shame, too! My life completely stopped, and his just kept going. As I sit here in the stands, I see it all unfold again right before my eyes, I'm there standing next to myself at the door. I'm watching from the other side of the room as he choked me, and proceeded to rape me by force. I was reliving it all over again, this time with my eyes wide open. I could see it all as the waves and splashes from the swimmers filled the background of my mind. Watching him ride pass my house, grinning at me, banishing me his gun. The coach yells, "Get off the bottom!" And it snaps my thoughts back to the boys' swimming lessons.

I can't imagine what I should do other than telling young women how to protect themselves, treasure their unique characteristics that make them who they are. I'm not the same person I was, I'm better, because now I'm stronger, and I will tell how I was date raped, not by a stranger but a friend.

Chapter 10: The Aftermath

Winter was almost at its end, and I wasn't happy about it. With the melting of the snow and the rain that would dry up all too soon meant terror for me. The change in season meant he would be back again floating on the summer's warm breeze to strike fear in me to keep me silent. Damon didn't want the neighborhood to find out the he was a rapist. Not only a rapist, but he raped one of his boy's cousins. Someone everyone liked and knew from a child. He would protect his self at all cost, and if that meant threatening and nearly beating my cousin to death, then so be it.

I stayed with James after the rape, and I keep my mouth shut. That was only for a short spell. He wanted to have sex, and I wasn't able mentally to have another man in me. So, that meant to do it or to tell what happened. I tried to keep my internal madness still, quiet within, endure, but I wasn't able to. James wanted to make love, I called it have sex because men don't look at the act like women do most of the time. When we tried, I yelled out "Damon don't!" My eyes opened wide and he looked at me strangely.

"Who in the hell is Damon?" He pulled away, and waited for me to speak. "Donna, did you hear me?"

"Yes" I began to tell him bits and pieces of the sordid event, I was ashamed not only of the rape but because I went out with another guy, laid in his bed and messed around, and tried to keep it hidden.

A long silence hung over and around us, we didn't speak for some time. He did hold me, and said "It would be okay." After a while, the questions came, "Where does he live? What does he drive and where does he parents live?"

"What are you going to do?"

"Nothing right now!" I knew that was a lie! The night was ended with a multitude of questions, and ugly comments. He promised we would stay together no matter what, and he would handle this guy for what he did to me.

I never knew what he was thinking, and when James made his mind up to do something he did it. He was fast tempered, but he was standing by me. I didn't know for how long, but for the time being he protected me from him. I moved in with him, and his mother was totally against it, she felt I was "damaged good" and would never in her eyes be good enough for her son. I understood it, but I didn't like it. I already thought badly of myself, and I didn't need anyone else adding to the load I was carrying.

Without me knowing James went to my cousin Dave and borrowed his car, he didn't tell him what for, but Dave gave it to him. That was the end of silence, because James went to Damon's parent's house and told his mother that he raped me. He told her everything that happened. How her son had been stalking me, about him pulling a gun on me, and that he threatened to kill me after the police called him.

James was on their front porch talking to his mother, and Damon was inside the house listening on the other side of the front door. Damon came out and he and James started fighting. Damon yelled to his mother, "Get the gun!" and his mother ran in to get it! Damon took it and pointed it at James. He looked him in his faces, and said "I'm going to kill you!" and he pulled the trigger! He was amazed that it didn't fire, because his mother had removed the bullets before she came back outside. James held up his hands and backed away. He drove off, and left them both in the front yard arguing about the incident. I couldn't believe this was all happening because of me. I was to blame, too.

My phone rang after several times, I picked up the receiver and it was my cousin Kevin on the other end. He never called me unless something was wrong, and it was. "Hello?"

"Dawn, Damon and five guys jumped on Dave at work, and beat him unconscious."

"What? When did this happen?"

My cousin said, "A few minutes ago."

I jumped in my car and headed up the street to the party store where he worked at. I was at my mom's house which was only three blocks away from the store, so I got there really fast. I could see the ambulance outside and on lookers were all about, trying to find out what happened. I jumped out the car, "Dave, are you alright?" He was sitting in the back of the EMS truck on the stretcher. His face was beaten to a bloody pulp, I started crying!

"Dee, Dee, it's okay. I'm okay." He always called me Dee. He was my favorite cousin, and we were the best of friends since we were little kids. I hate to say this beating was the end of our closeness. Things were never the same for us after this.

I lost so much! I lost my dignity, my respect from my family, and myself. I was hurting and I hurt a lot of people in the process, and it was something I never meant to do. I was a broken bird that couldn't fly, and my relationship with everyone had changed. My family looked at me differently because of what happened to my cousin. I hoped it didn't lead to someone else getting hurt or killed.

What I learned later was the incident between James and Damon wasn't the first. James went to his home one night and confronted him about raping me, and he denied everything, but before he opened the door he had called the police. Damon didn't come outside until the police pulled up. James explained to the police what happened and why he was there. James told me that the police asked him to leave, but they too would have confronted the men who had raped someone they knew. Damon wanted James to try something; it would give him a valid reason for killing him in his front yard. It would have been trespassing, and it could be a justified murder.

I can't believe how seeing him brought these unpleasant memories or recollections forth, because of a random run in with the man who raped me twenty years ago. I hate remembering all of this! I hate how it makes me feel, and I remember how I was alone because my family felt like maybe I lied about the rape all because I liked him.

To this day I never asked why they treated me the way they did, and I never really wanted to know. I'm forty-two years old now and it's time for me to release what I have hidden away from the world. Being raped is something you never really get over with, it just dims like a light until it's turned back on. Well the lights were turned on, and I'm ready to confront it forever, and the only way to do it is to confront the demon face on. I am happy that I finally have the courage to stand up and say what really happened that September night twenty years ago.

Chapter 11: The Now

Here it is the second week of January, and my daughter I conceived with James nineteen years earlier is on her way back to college to start her second semester. I am so proud of her; she is a beautiful young lady. I think she's one of the best things I have ever done. James and I briefly talked, but mostly argue about tuition monies, and him helping out more with her college education. I must say he has been a great father to her, but he just wasn't a good husband for me. James and I stayed together for seven years. We eventually grew apart, because most men can't overlook things like women do. We take our experiences whether good or bad and mode them into something positive to move on to. Men hold on to what they know about women and resent them for it.

Although our marriage didn't last long, he will always be my first for many reasons. I am married to my second husband and after many troubled years together he has become my soul mate. I finally found it! We share our home with our two sons and his stepdaughter.

This past holiday season has made me think about things differently. I want things to be a lot smoother in my life, and it's important for that to happen given the emotional upset I experienced seeing my attacker again. I am almost back to normal now, but I still look in all the cars driving on the side of me. I am not as afraid as I was. I think for my own mental stability, writing this book has done me a world of good-being able to talk about what happened to me, and what might happen to other women if they aren't careful.

I hope that this book will help other women come forward and confront their attackers and shake loose the bond of fear that holds them. I am liberating myself from it as well. I am looking forward and I don't want to look back anymore. The next step in my liberation will be to confront my attacker face to face; I want to know why he did this to me. I want him to admit what he did to me was wrong!

Have you any idea how many women are walking around the city, from state to state who has been raped, staked, beaten, or abused? The findings are amazing-at least women today have the Date Rape Law that was passed in 2000 by President Clinton, and any person who forces a woman to have sexual intercourse can be punished by the court of law and it could carry a sentence of up to twenty years. I was date raped years before, but I am thankful that some form of protection is in place to help other women.

Women are subjected to many things in this world, and with every turn or glance there are predators around us in some form or another. The predators are our neighbors, friends, and acquaintances. These men lurk in the shadows of our existence and they plan to destroy us, women who think highly about themselves, women who are independent, and move to a different beat. That was me: strong, beautiful, and carefree. He took all that from me, but I want it back!

I think back to the times I spoke to a rape counselor to understand why this man I knew since I was ten years old date raped me, and my counselor told me that I was lucky. Most men who rape women tend to kill the women that they are familiar with. They want to keep their secret, and with us both knowing each other, it would be hard to keep it from getting out in the open. He told me he would kill me if I ever told, and I believed that after the rape, stalking and terrifying me. He tried to kill my cousin, and here I am trying to release myself from this internal torment that I have carried all these years. I found myself riding pass the drug store looking for the white pick-up. I'm hoping to catch a glimpse of him, and his truck. I am going to confront him after all these years. I want to get it out in the open. I want to know why he raped me! This would help me finally finish this chapter in the book, and close it and place it on the shelf. I want to be free of my memories of him, the rape, and the terror I feel when I see him. It's February now, and spring will arrive in a few short months, and I'll be waiting for him.

The second half of my life will be greater than the first. I won't be afraid to walk through my neighborhood with my children in fear of running into him.

> **Job 42:10, 12** *"After Job had prayed for his friends, and the-Lord gave him twice as much as he had before. The Lord blessed the latter part of Job's life more than the first."*

I want to free myself from all the things that hurt at this point of my life, and sharing my story with the world is going to do just that. This is my story, this is the burden I have carried with me for twenty years and it has almost killed me.

I am finally in a place in my life where I'm happy and content with my surroundings. I went on and graduated from college with a Bachelor's Degree in Liberal Arts and a Master's Degree in Teaching. I am wonderfully made, and the Lord has blessed me with many positive people around me that will continue to enrich my life forever. This is my story, I was date raped not by a stranger but a friend!

Chapter 12

If you read this book and find yourself in a familiar place, that place where you have stored away things that scared, hurt, and maybe even nearly destroyed you; then now is the time for you to find closure. Just let go of all that has pained you in the past, just understand that it's going to be a lengthy process, but just reflect of this scripture as you make you journey:

> **Proverbs: 3:5-6,** *"Trust in the Lord with all thine heart: and lean not unto thine own understanding. In all thy ways acknowledge him, and he shall direct thy paths."*

This scripture says it all to me; you need to lean on God's understanding of things, and not on your own. Not mine and not yours, His. Once you do this, much will be revealed to you. I know from experience what God can do for you. He has changed me, saved me, and will continue to love me. This I am a witness too, because God has done it my entire life.

This is where my journey starts, by confessing His goodness and strength that I have been blessed with to tell my story. Not to fear what others will think, but to help those that are holding the same secret I held all these years to just let go! Free yourself, and take back your life. Seek help and, you can do this by contacting the site below.

If you are survivor of sexual abuse please contact: **RAINN-Rape Crisis Center at 1800-656-HOPE (4673)**, or log on to www.rainn.org for more confidential assistance, 24/7.

I only hope that I helped women of any age to take back their power.

Philippians: 1:6, *"Being confident of this very thing, that He which hath begun a good work in you will perform it until that day of Jesus Christ."*

I know first-hand that God has begun a good work in me, and He will bring me through to completion in His time.